A Bit of Applause for Mrs. Claus

Susie Schick-Pierce, Jeannie Schick-Jacobowitz,

Muffin Drake-Policastro

Illustrated by Wendy Wallin Malinow

sourcebooks
jabberwocky

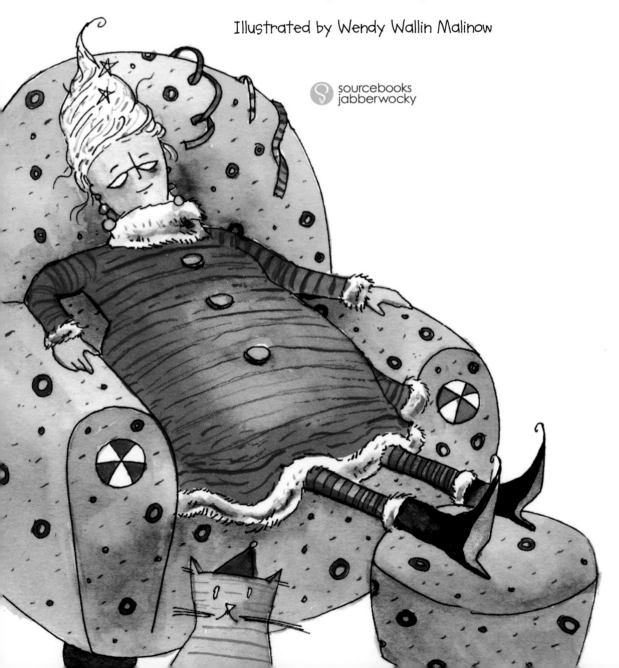

Copyright © 2012 by Susie Schick-Pierce, Jeannie Schick-Jacobowitz, Muffin Drake-Policastro
Cover and internal design © 2012 by Sourcebooks, Inc.
Cover design by Julie Neely
Illustrations © 2012 by Wendy Wallin Malinow

Sourcebooks and the colophon are registered trademarks of Sourcebooks, Inc.

Published by Sourcebooks Jabberwocky, an imprint of Sourcebooks, Inc.
P.O. Box 4410, Naperville, Illinois 60567-4410
(630) 961-3900
Fax: (630) 961-2168
www.sourcebooks.com

CIP data is on file with the publisher.

Source of production: Leo Paper, Heshan City, Guangdong Province, China
Date of production: September 2012
Run number: 17860

Printed and bound in China.
LEO 10 9 8 7 6 5 4 3 2 1

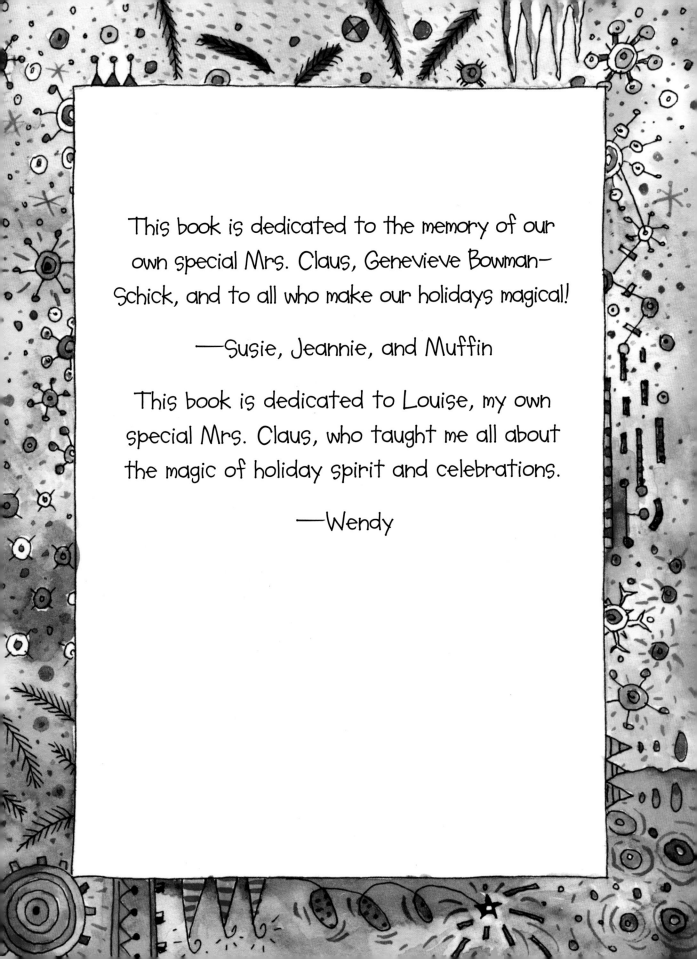

This book is dedicated to the memory of our own special Mrs. Claus, Genevieve Bowman-Schick, and to all who make our holidays magical!

—Susie, Jeannie, and Muffin

This book is dedicated to Louise, my own special Mrs. Claus, who taught me all about the magic of holiday spirit and celebrations.

—Wendy

It's the day
before Christmas,
But Santa's sick
with the flu!

Mrs. Claus
has a problem:

"There's still
so much to do!"

First she dashes
off letters
On Santa's long list.

Then she trims
all the trees

And decks the halls
that were missed.

She wraps the
last presents.
The elves help out, too.

Yikes!

The cookies are burned!

What a hullabaloo!

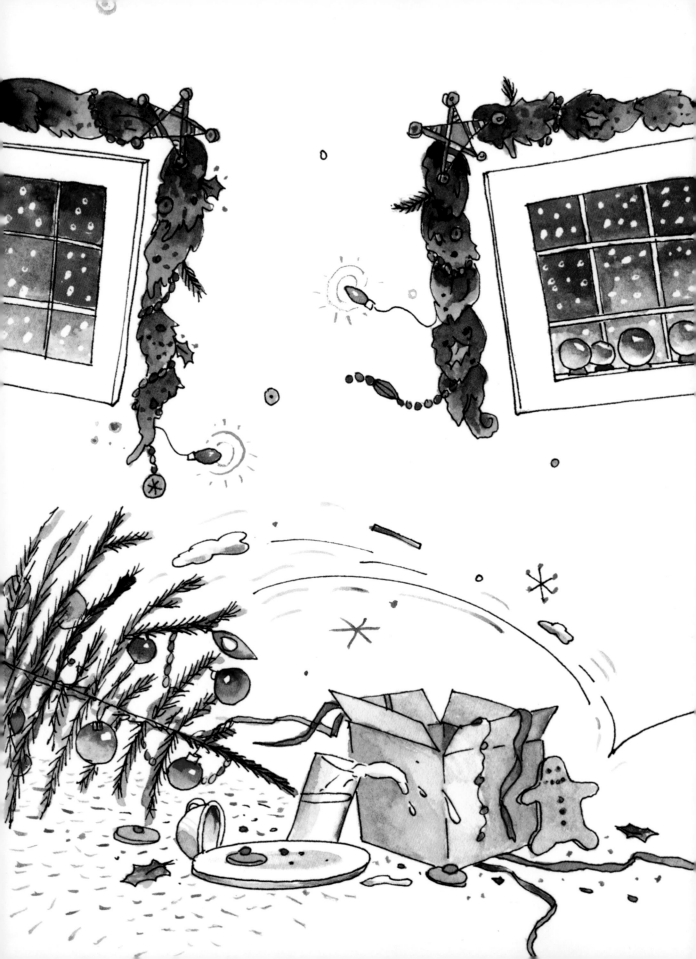

Mrs. Claus
goes to leave,
but she trips
over trash.

Down goes the
tree with a big
giant CRASH!

Next,
to the reindeer.

It's almost time
for the ride.

"Come Dancer,
Come Prancer..."

Soon they're right
by her side.

They leap to
the rooftop,
For take-off's
at nine.

But, what's that?
It's Santa!
He's feeling
just fine!

Mrs. Claus puts
her feet up
As they fly
out of sight.

A Bit of Applause for

Mrs. Claus!

She saved

Christmas tonight!

MERRY

And one last thought
Before the
book's through.